GRAB HOLD THE DUST

GRAB HOLD THE DUST

by

Darris

factotum

Sierra Vista, AZ

factotum books, published in Sierra Vista, AZ, are available at Amazon.com and other retailers.

factotum2010@live.com

CONTENTS

En Ami

"If I'm truly as weird as you claim I am, why do you waste your precious time working, and living, with me?" Igneous asked and slid her chair out from under our table. She stood up swiftly and caught the edge of her black lace dress on one of her two-inch heels. Her dress was pulled downward immediately, revealing her bare body underneath. This problem didn't seem to faze her at first, and she pulled her dress back up with her arms crisscrossed over her chest. As she looked from Tom toward me, I noticed small tears gathering in the corners of her small, dark, almost mouse-like eyes. She only glanced at me for a moment though, just long

1

enough to regain her composure. "And here," she said, "take this to remember me by!" She then hurled a leaf of crisp lettuce from her plate at Tom, and stormed outside while the creamy Italian dressing from her salad splattered into a tiny Milky Way on the left lapel of Tom's jacket.

"Damn it!" Tom bellowed, trying to rub the dressing, and apparently, his jacket out of existence. Tom was an enormous man whose actions always seemed strikingly pointed. He liked the idea of getting things done, and didn't mince words in trying to do so. "There," he said, and the stain was no more. "Always so over emotional..." He paused as he tried to curtail the slight grin on his face which had just then caught his attention. I could tell that he thought the whole situation was hilarious. "She gets that way when I mention my ex-wife and our 'traditional' relationship. I'm not sure why. As she likes to point out, there was absolutely no cause for a marriage between myself and Diane. It was just something to do at the time."

"Why'd you mention Diane then?" I asked.

"Well, what the hell else am I supposed to talk about with an old buddy like you? Most of our times together involved Diane and Louise. How's she doin' anyway?"

"I'm not really sure," I said. "Last I heard she was in Houston working for a P.R. firm -- ironic isn't it? As Igneous so eloquently puts it there wasn't ever any cause for a marriage between us either, so we went our separate ways about a year ago. No hardships involved."

"C'est la vie," Tom said and ordered our second bottle of Chateau Godineau. It seemed as if once again we were on our own, getting drunk and laughing at our own past stupidity, telling each other exaggerated stories.

I couldn't hold it in any longer so I decided to ask about Igneous twenty minutes later into the night. It had been ten years since we had separated and the 'Tom-and-Jerry Express' had derailed and broken many hearts in the Greater New Orleans area, and all I knew about my once best buddy was his address and the fact that he had been living with a gorgeous and up-and-coming model, namely Igneous, ten years his junior, for three of those ten years. Tom looked quite puzzled by my inquiry and began rubbing his overly bushy black eyebrows backwards, making each hair stand up separately like little soldiers at attention. I remembered that he used to always do this, as if to emphasize the increase in his thought processes.

"I hope you're not worried about Igneous," he said. "She always does this when we go out with old friends of mine. It's like a pseudo-sexual game with her. She storms out or gets angry with everybody just so we can make up later at home. At least this time we were able to finish part of our dinners first." Tom laughed heartily aloud just as the waiter presented me with the night's check.

Tom said, "Let me get that," and snatched the check from my still outstretched hand. "We've provided the impromptu theatrics so we might as well go all the way and pay the bill too." How generous I thought; much more generous than I ever remember him having been in the past. As we both stood up to leave, Tom reached across the table, knocking the table's center candle down, and put his broad hands on my shoulders.

"Merry Christmas," he belched in four syllables into my astonished face. His breath stank of stale wine and fettuccine. How drunk I thought. I remembered him being that way. I picked up the candle while Tom exited out of the restaurant and onto St. Charles Ave.

I heard Tom's grunting before I even opened the door to leave. "She took my goddamned car!" he turned around and yelled at me.

"Don't worry," I said, "I'll take you home in my car." We got in and drove down St. Charles talking the entire way about the old days when I used to drive everyone around in the back of my 'monster truck' as he called it, a huge '74 Chevy convertible.

"Those were some good times," he said. "Remember when we climbed over the walls of the old stadium to see the Tulane vs. USC game? Man, what a blast!" Tom was extremely animated when drunk and his body movements shook my car wildly. "Turn here!" he screamed suddenly, "Turn here!" We were at the intersection of St. Charles and Broadway, so I took a right as he commanded.

It startled and amazed me that he still had so much energy. I wanted to ask him how he kept so lively but he always had something else to reminisce about. While he spoke I drove slowly and looked around at all the people on Broadway, running from bar to bar and from house to house. I guessed that there were about twice as many as when Tom and I went to college. Tom suddenly fell silent. I looked over and he too was staring out of the window. "Stop here," he directed.

"Where? We're not at your house yet," I said. He was already opening the car door. I slammed on the brake pedal and he stumbled out into the middle of the street.

"Go park the car," he said with his head turned firmly away from me, "I'll meet you inside *The Boot*." I was annoyed at his childish arrogance in assuming that I wanted to participate in this adventure. I closed his door and parked the car only to go retrieve him, take him home, and end the night.

The Boot was the college bar which was firmly stuck in my mind as being *The Barn* during Tom's and my heyday. Maybe I was mistaken. Anyway, Tom was now in there amidst volumes of permed hair and miles and miles of stretched denim, and I had to go get him. The Barn, or Boot, had never been much to talk about, except for the fact that everybody always seemed to be there. That much hadn't changed and it was obviously

8

'Rush Week' at the fraternities because the people were overflowing out of the open glass doors of the bar, onto the street corner, and into the street. I hadn't been bar-hopping in the ten years since I dropped out of Tulane my sophomore year and joined the Army. I had many opportunities to go out to bars mind you, in many foreign countries, the military is famous for that after all, but I always declined. As I waded through the crowds of people I remembered why: I just plain hated it. I only went to bars while in college because there wasn't anything else to do. Quiet, more personal functions like dinner parties were more my style, but they seemed to occur only later in life. To put it simply, I enjoyed the quieter years and appreciated them remaining that way.

After five or ten minutes of struggling, I reached the bar and started looking around. To get a better view of my surroundings I stepped up onto the foot railing which ran the length of the bar. "What is this old guy doing?" everyone around me was probably thinking. Luckily, I spotted Tom in no time, over in the corner with the pool tables. He appeared to have two young coeds enthralled with his old glory stories. I hadn't noticed until then but Tom presented an almost overwhelming image. His large frame was at least twice as big as anyone present, even bigger than I remembered him being in college. Standing an impressive six feet six inches and weighing two hundred and eighty pounds, Tom dominated the room.

It looked like Tom was playing that old scam of his where he told women he'd met that he played for the so-and-so football team. I know because I could see him flexing his muscles; it couldn't have been anything else.

Of course, they always fell for it because he was humongous. What they didn't know was that Tom knew absolutely nothing about the game of football, and never had. Oh, he loved to watch it alright. He enjoyed the crunching and bashing, but somehow it never occurred to him that he should play. He most likely would have been extremely good at it. In college he liked the fact that he could just tell girls that he played and get what he called the 'fringe benefits' of a vast and hearty gene pool.

Tom didn't appear too thrilled when he finally noticed me approaching. And why should he be happy to see me? Because I was there to save him from himself, that's why. I had been calling out his name during the time that I was trying to get through this second group of people inside the bar, but it was obvious that he couldn't hear me through the din they were making. He could see me though, because I was the only person in the bar who was headed in a definite direction, besides those patrons headed for the restrooms. The closer I went, the closer he appeared to move toward the girls. When I finally reached them, Tom had one girl under each arm and he was smiling, with inch after inch of his enormous white teeth showing. The girls giggled beneath him.

"Larry... Good ole Larry... Let me introduce you to a couple of good friends of mine..."

"Tom," I interrupted, "my name is Jerry. Can I speak with you for a minute?" He said some apologies to the girls and came closer to me. "What the hell are you doing? Look, I haven't seen you for years but the Thomas Phillipe that I knew would not be doing this." He asked me to repeat myself because he couldn't understand me with all the noise. I raised my voice to a level that I'm sure his two new girlfriends could also hear. "What about Igneous?" I shouted. "Don't you think she's been hurt and embarrassed enough tonight?" Tom rubbed the five o'clock shadow under his chin and sucked his teeth. My God, I thought, tell me -- Is it me or him? Which one of us is it? Who's crazy here? He had thought about what I said for less than a minute when he replied.

"Igneous can take care of herself," he said. "She's been doin' it for twenty years. Anyway Jerry, these two young ladies here have invited us to the Delta Gamma Rush Party; it's goin' on right now. Interested?"

"No." I turned around to leave disappointed and realizing for the first time that night that the whole situation was hopeless. Tom still wanted to be a teenager and I was nothing more than a stranger in this environment now. I didn't know the rules in my own home town anymore, and was pretty happy about it as I quietly exited the bar, flanked on all sides by blossoming youth.

DETERMINATION

I know a girl, who is so amorous and so loving, that she

sends

all of her scabs to me via the U.S. mail.

She says that they are crunchy.

She says she wants to give herself to me completely.

She sends clumps of her hair wrapped in rubber bands

and toe and fingernail clippings,

curled and dry and hard as coconut husks.

There, that discolored spot on the letter, she writes in a

frantic stream-of-consciousness fashion, that is my day

condensed

to one single, salty tear.

If life and circumstances won't let me have her whole,

she

writes, then I should have her piece by piece by piece.

perilous

for you

I'll craft this fairy tale

and see it through

to its conclusion

forgetting everything past

as though its existence

were just a dream

meant to fade

as I awoke within your eyes

but to make it real

you have to believe in the magic

without your will

I won't be able to find my way

the tale will crash

silently into the mountainside

careening softly

towards the shrouded valley

below

days in afghan

when my feet wobble at the ankles

as I step from rock to rock

I don't stop to try and steady myself,

I know that would be fruitless

my flat feet give way

to the terrain beneath them

because they must

So I trundle on, undaunted

once in my office

I, alone, refuse to punch the clock

19

I sip coffee after coffee

aware of those who surround me

aware of my circumstance

they gather together because

they want the strength of the many

while I radiate my power from within

they feel it, but don't understand

what makes me so confident?

how do I flaunt their rules,

and get away with it?

why am I so young and energetic

when we are all chronologically

almost the same age?

they don't understand that I have

already tasted death

so life holds no sway over me

I have told them this, mind you

they just choose not to believe

out for dinner

eating at an Italian restaurant

seven of us

I, the only man

how ineffectual you feel

with six women around

you would think you'd feel

masculine, emboldened, macho even

but that is far from

the feeling that that situation

manufactures

instead you feel

small, effeminate, unable

or unwilling to make

decisions

even for yourself.

PTO2

Although they weren't as good as beers, I was determined to get drunk off something every night before class PTO2 started; it really didn't matter to me that my only choice was straight orange juice. I had to drink something to make me forget what a wild and free life I led as a civilian. Besides, alternating current circuits weren't too interesting on an empty stomach. After six pints of O.J. I could pretend to be drunk by myself, and sway back and forth in my chair to the rhythm and sloshing deep inside my body.

"What the hell are you doing, Thompson?" asked SFC Callahan. "I see you back there with your eyes closed; bullshitting. If you'd pay attention every once and awhile you might actually learn something. You'd be surprised."

"Sergeant," I said with a look so in-control it almost scared me, "I was paying you the utmost of attention. The only reason I closed my eyes was to get a better mental image of the circuit you were discussing." The class as a whole, four others besides me, chuckled a bit as I kept my face as straight as possible. They could smell bullshit a mile away, and I knew that, but when the opportunity arose it seemed incredibly easy to entertain them. If you didn't really like the idea of life in the military you might say they were a true captive audience. We had all volunteered to be there, but it was certainly the only voluntary thing I had ever done in my life that I couldn't just quit when I had had enough. They had us for keeps.

The first night of class was okay enough. Or rather, as okay as any first night of a course you didn't want to be in, could be. At least now we all were used to the late hours of a night schedule, and sleeping in class was cut down to a minimum from class PTO1. Sergeant Dickwood, a former semi-pro halfback, or so he claimed, was automatically named Class Leader because of his rank. This didn't surprise me, or my fellow privates, but it was extremely hard to stomach his 'better than thou because of rank' attitude, when his average was the lowest of anyone who passed the introductory course. He blamed that ugly fact on his inability to learn effectively from the computer used for the B.E.S.T. program, Basic Electronic Skills Tester. The SGT claimed his scores would dramatically increase with an

26

instructor. I was once again named Assistant Class Leader by SGT Dickwood who apparently liked my general attitude and performance. I still haven't been able to figure out why he liked me; I was the only one who had verbally stated that I didn't want to be in class, or the 33P (Electronic Intercept Strategic Receiving Subsystem Repairer) MOS for that matter.

On the second night when our long nine o'clock to nine thirty break was over, the privates slowly re-entered the building for class. Most had been downstairs in the snack area, bumming for change to religiously place into vending machines which held such items as: candy bars, chips, microwave popping corn, apples, oranges, burritos, cold sandwiches, and of course Reese's Peanut Butter Cups. Fake fights would break out at least once a week, before the machines were refilled, over

27

who ate at last of the Peanut Butter Cups. I usually had. And I'd usually win the fake fights.

The student NCOs hung out in a separate part of the building after they bought their junk food. They apparently didn't want to appear as if they were as low as the rest of us. We talked about them back in class. They were always five minutes longer with their breaks.

"...and I'd sure like to tell SGT Dickwood what I really thought about him," said Krumrie, the sergeant's favorite target for correction. "I'd say, 'Fuck you Dickhead, I didn't join the Army to hear about Regulation 600-32 dealing with punishment given out for putting your legs up on a desk. I joined for the educational benefits." Once I had overheard Dickwood say he wanted to be a 33, electronic technician and repairman, to build a 'Death Tank'. I decided not to mention this because I figured he already looked stupid enough. I didn't have to help. "It's shitty," Krumrie continued, "when any NCO's in a class, because they seem to forget the fact that they're students too. Just like us."

"Who cares if they've had a previous MOS and more military experience," added Saw, a chubby balding private. I couldn't decide if he was being sarcastic or not.

"I certainly don't care," Krumrie said. "He has to prove that he has the right to order me around. Until then I'll give him as much grief as possible."

"But if you start messing up in class, like not knowing how to do some of the problems, he probably won't go out of his way to help you."

"If I ever need help from him I'll kill myself."

"I wouldn't go that far," I interrupted, "but that

29

would be a very sad day when any of us needed help from SGT Dickwood."

"Would it now?" asked SFC Callahan as he stood up from behind his instructor's desk at the front of the room. He had been back there the entire time, checking the wiring of a multimeter by attaching each lead to a separate exposed wire. He had the usual teacher-to-student look on his face, a stern and demanding look. You never knew if he was angry or not. He bent back down to detach the multimeter and his now disembodied voice was heard throughout the classroom, "You guys have something against SGT Dickwood?"

"I don't," said Saw quickly.

Krumrie stared in the direction of the chalkboard. He seemed to be debating with himself whether or not to speak up. "I do," he said in a whisper. At that SFC

Callahan stood up and unrolled his BDU sleeves. He looked more at ease than he had before.

"I do too," I said.

"I don't like him much myself. He's too annoying and always tells those stupid dirty jokes to try and fit in." We all laughed, Sergeant Callahan the most. I liked that class much more then. "Once," he said, "I even heard him say he wanted to build some sort of 'Death Tank' with what he learned here. I said, 'Man, you crazy! You don't learn nothing like that here. You're just a repairman. Don't try and go overboard.' Man, you should've seen him then! He shut right up." SFC Callahan was almost in hysterics with laughter. "Don't get me wrong," he finally composed himself and said, "he's an alright guy, just a little misdirected."

"And intense," Saw said.

31

I had to correct him - "You mean extreme."

Right then SGT Dickwood entered the classroom and everyone, including SFC Callahan became quiet. Dickwood walked slowly past Krumrie, stopped at me and stood staring. He said, "What's extreme, Thompson?" with a crooked smirk on his lips.

"You, Sergeant," I said. "We were just sitting here for the last five minutes discussing your life."

"Sure you were."

"I swear. Ask anyone sergeant."

He reached over and fixed my collar, stepped back sizing me up, stepped forward again and adjusted my left E-2/PV2 mosquito wings. I noticed he smelled a bit like cigarettes and Ben-Gay® muscle rub combined. "No... I... Well it doesn't really matter," he said and resumed walking to his seat. SFC Callahan coughed loudly, directing our attention his way. Quietly, SGT Dickwood took his chair out from under his desk and sat down. "Maybe I'll have to try and get back sooner from break."

"Maybe you should," Krumrie said.

"Maybe we should all get back to electronics," said SFC Callahan.

We did, and SGT Dickwood didn't speak to anyone for the rest of the night. The few times that he even turned toward us anyone who cared to observe could see that his cheeks were flushed and what appeared to be a tear sat trapped between his lashes on the outside corner of his right eye. He never made a move to wipe it away. He probably understood that any movement he made to hide his pain would draw our attention and most likely make things that much harder

33

for him. He was right, too. While I sat quietly studying his reactions to a different Army than he had previously known, already somewhat at peace with my own loneliness, I'm sure that if any of our fellow classmates would have noticed his suffering they would have never stopped talking about the time that SGT Dickwood cried in class.

I actually felt sorry for him at that moment. I got the distinct impression that he was one of those people who tried mightily to always make friends with their co-workers. He had chosen the wrong MOS for that, though. While 33s were some of the smartest, or the smartest, soldiers in the Army, they were also renowned for their lack of social skills. It was as if SGT Dickwood had wandered into Comic-Con® and had repeatedly tried to start up a conversation about the last Tyson fight. He was not used to being the odd man out, and it showed.

cancer

there is a stillness

in an old house in Europe

unlike the stillness you will ever

feel in any house in America,

no matter what its age

or its history.

this is a stillness

born of thousands of years

of human existence

bedded down for the night,

locked away

from the known madness

that comes with the moon.

I don't remember kissing that little girl

at some party

where guys shout anthems,

"throw that 'd',"

"fight the power,"

"kick it to me, g..."

I sway

not dance

drinking heavily

despite my meager weight

I say, "it must

go all to my breasts,

my nipples are hard."

truly,

they've never been harder

later I reach

consciousness

embraced by another

girl

whose nipples,

between my astonished fingers,

are raised

petrified in ecstasy

we remain together,

ever so tenderly,

only a minute more

her small lips

barely gracing mine

with touch

separate,

but transfixed,

we stare

while re-adjusting our blouses

she rises and leaves

and I re-enter the party

nine guys crowd around

as I sit on the couch

each, in succession

asking me to dance

"no thank you,"

I say,

"my nipples

are not aroused."

one long drive

the horizon

greets me second by second

but still I refuse

to arrive

I don't remember being

such a bad guest before

I was the one to always

smile and say "hello"

to extend my hand

but lately, I've been

much more hesitant

everyday used to hold

what I thought were

infinite possibilities

but now the horizon

mocks me with its beauty

we both know

that the thrill is in the chase

at the destination

is only darkness

and the end of the ride

Munich

if you're young

that last drop of the darkest beer

you have ever seen, or tasted,

coating the inside of the noisy

tent, a thick caramel,

giving your one liter stein a

liquid consistency,

making every lonely mädchen

a goddess

birthed only to nurture your

progeny,

making her flesh a malleable putty,

firm against your fingers,

is perhaps the last thing you'll

remember about Munich

besides the polizei's

spring-mounted baton.

CHAMOIS

As he walked away from the disputed apartment, from the corner of his eye a strange object in the sky caught his attention. Despite his festering anger he looked, quickly but intently. The smallness of the object and the way its lateral distance matched its acceleration toward the earth was odd and perplexed him.

Abruptly, he recognized the fast-moving silhouette of a man and his terror propelled him back toward his door, which was slightly ajar.

She left her resentment of him and his ignorantly harsh words back between the sofa where she was previously seated and the antique chair from Germany.

He yanked her outside by the arm in such a manner that she knew he had forgotten all about their earlier argument.

Outside they stood together in a desperate embrace, closer than they had been in months. They located the still falling speck of a man, arms and legs visibly spread eagle.

Please have some sort of chute, she said.

They both remembered their last trip toward the Zugspitze, up their favorite gorge in the Alps. The beautiful old chamois, which fell to the granite ledge a thousand feet below, had established an unbreakable emotional bond between them. She was glad that connection was there and they could always fall back on it, but she was also saddened by its apparent necessity. At the last moment they looked away simultaneously, their hearts conjoined and constricted.

I'm desperate, I'm weak, and I'm alone

I am desperate

more desperate than I'd ever imagined

to control my emotions

takes an amount of willpower

that I obviously just don't have

I am weak

weaker than the youngest newborn babe

they are stronger by far,

society has yet to manipulate them

instill in them the fear that is necessary to survive

I am alone

finally and forever alone

I've realized this

as eventually we all do

and consequently it's made me desperate.

too lazy to name this

everything if you persist

at it, becomes easier and easier, until

it's so easy that it becomes

hard to maintain the intensity

with which you had began

I've learned to hold back

to not begin

to procrastinate whenever

I have the time

to wait until others do

what I had only dreamt about.

51

that way, any disappointments

belong solely to them

but, we can share any victories.

chasers

when all hell broke loose

I trusted myself and stood stone still

I glimpsed the panicked faces and eyes

of those around me

I chose tranquility, even though it was not on the menu

were the enemy near

I would leap into action as required

but he was nowhere in sight

his handiwork triggered by a timer

only comrades and co-workers

crisscrossed from bunker to bunker

each swift to where another had been

none going in any specific direction

I remembered how in my youth

sadly named firecrackers

only seemed to chase those who ran

Humanity

I see an unfinished sculpture,

The Unfinished Head I think it's called,

or maybe Half of Head, I can't remember.

A mockery of sculpture or a mockery of life

or, just maybe, the whole of personality.

Unfinished or halved, whatever it may be,

it is there so we must accept it

This mockery of sculpture defies all nature.

It is not whole, only unsure. It is not stable but dynamic

Some call it whole and finished, and also magnificent.

Some say the

sculptor made a mistake in finishing it and call it

disgusting. Some call it only

human.

Good Sex

"Why not?" I thought to myself. "Why not fuck an animal?" Some of the humans I had sex with had come extremely close to being animals. They were always very quick to associate any sexual act they were about to indulge in with some type of animal. "Let's do it doggy style," she'd say, or ' Let's play horsy, cowboy," or "Lick my cat," or "Bust my beaver." It seemed as if I had been in bed with animals my whole life. Maybe I had been, but it still wasn't easy to hear other men have a conversation about it in public. It was a subject that only southern men could talk about with such revelry.

"Yeah man, but those sheep are easy. You gotta

57

know how to fuck a chicken!" one man said. They all began laughing obnoxiously loud. "I couldn't handle no feathers on my dick," he finished. His friends laughed aloud again, disturbing the only woman on the ferry landing. She was noticeably uneasy about the whole situation.

"I've been at sea so long," a second man said, "so long that I can smell a woman." He looked over at me then. I expected him to point at me and exclaim, "There's a woman in disguise! I can smell her." All he did, though, was to walk over to me and repeat his previous statement. "I can smell a woman," he said.

"I know what you mean," I replied.

He said, "No, you don't understand. I mean I can smell when they want to have sex; when they're in heat." He turned away to face his friends, and then back again.

"I've been aboard, off the coast of Lebanon for six months straight. I can smell a woman." I wondered if Lebanon had a coast. I was about to ask when he continued. "You going to work across the river?" he asked. I said no. "You work on the Westbank?" Again I answered no. "Oh, you're going to go party and pick up some chicks, huh?" This time I agreed. "Sure am," I said. He placed his hand on my shoulder and announced to his three friends, "Now here's a man I like. Go get 'em!"

The ferry docked and we were all loaded aboard. It was the Alvin T. Stumpf, the large one, so I was quite confident that I wouldn't have to speak to this group of men again. They stayed upstairs, their loud voices echoing throughout the empty middle deck. I went downstairs to look out over the waves. Laughter followed me down the stairwell.

As the ferry pushed through the river, the waves which struck the bow danced in rhythm to the wakes of passing ships. The Mississippi, for once, looked relatively clean, its water a pleasant mold green, instead of its normal sand-colored, soupy brown. I was caught up in trying to interpret the motions of the waves as words, when an apparently middle-aged man who looked to be the typical vagrant type, approached me and began speaking. "I was once hard like you, my man. I mean hard. I was so hard I had women all on my jock! You know what I'm sayin'? Women would call me up day an' night. My phone never sat still. I'd go out to bars like you." I nodded in agreement even though I wasn't sure if he knew I was even there. "I'd find one of my girls," he said, "and, you know there'd be some other homeboy I

60

had to show what time it was and then I'd take my girl back to where she stayed at an' do what I wanted. You know what I mean? I'll tell ya though, I shouldn't have married her. I'm tellin' ya, don't do it. Her booty's all wavy and flappin' na. I don't wanna fuck that shit." He stopped talking and left just as abruptly as he had come. All I could do was laugh to myself. I wondered why people felt they should tell me those things.

The ferry docked on the Eastbank at Canal Street. When the ramps came down we unloaded. I noticed that the first four men that had spoken to me were still up to their conversation. They seemed to be able to laugh at each other forever. The bum who rambled on downstairs was nowhere to be seen. I hoped he wasn't driving a car.

I walked down Canal Street toward the streetcar

stop, whistling the entire way. I felt good for some reason. I waited at the stop for fifteen minutes and decided that, hell, I might as well walk to Lee Circle to wait for the streetcar. It was only about a half-mile away, and it sure beat Canal Street. Lee Circle was much quieter; less people.

I arrived at Lee Circle about twenty minutes later and sat down on the pavement. I was still feeling pretty good when a man, kind of short and chubby, like an earth-fallen cherub, rode up on his bike and asked me where he could find air for his rear tire. It was looking flat so I told him. "See that gas station right behind you," I said, "to the left, next to bushes, are the air and water hoses." He said thank you rode over there. Two minutes went by and he returned. He said, "Look, I'm not going to beat around the bush. I'm gay and I like your style. I like the way you speak too. I don't know if you're gay or not, but I bet you have a big thing. I'll pay you thirty bucks to let me suck your thing." I always thought I'd know what to say if someone gay approached me with such an offer. I thought I could pick the homosexuals out of a crowd. I would say something like, Fuck you faggot, or Fuck off; I was definitely homophobic. I found out that I didn't know what to say though.

"No... No...," I said. That's all I said. I stood still, looking down, and saying no. He eventually took the hint and left. I felt embarrassed.

The streetcar arrived and I paid my fare and sat down in front like usual. Everyone in the car had to look my way and I didn't like that at that moment, so I got up and moved to the absolute rear of the streetcar. I sat in the swivel chair that the conductor uses when the car is traveling in the opposite direction. I felt better back there, away from any inquiring eyes.

At the stop across the street from Melissa's house on South Carrollton, I got off the streetcar. I told the driver thank you as I exited out onto the neutral ground grass. The streetcar's doors almost closed on me. Melissa's door was a much welcomed sight. I knocked and Melissa emerged with a huge smile on her face. "How're you doing my big, sexy man?" she asked as she hugged and kissed me.

"Please, please, don't talk about sex," I said, "talk about anything else but sex."

"What's the matter?" she asked.

"I've just heard enough about sex today, that's all.

I'll tell you when it's good to talk about sex."

"Making love is always good to do or to talk about," she said.

"Not tonight it isn't," I replied. We went inside and sat down on the couch. "I'll tell you why later," I said. "Today is not a good day for sex."

grab hold the dust

tighter, world, tighter

squeeze me tighter!

grab hold the dust

I rose from it

to it I'll return

constrict and watch me

slip away

moist

my girlfriend hates the word "moist"

she says it reminds her of sex

I asked her what was wrong with sex

she said nothing was wrong with ours

it's just sex between others

that bothers her mind

I tell her that her moist lips

remind me of the morning grass

moist with dew

she cringes and cowers in the corner of the room

I tell her how a piece of moist cheesecake fat and dense

and creamy

moistens my taste buds

and she curls into a ball the size of a large globe

from the floor she asks

why I torture her with that evil word

I tell her it's because

she was asking me to.

That Perfect Smell

Clouds of joy

Drift by my silent window

Indifferent to the chatter

From jealous blue sky

Pregnant with rain

They gather and commingle

Gliding toward the inevitable,

Bellies full to bursting

Newly Found Love

I jump

I fall instead of fly or do I?

Feet lift and float

Both destined to feel earth again,

somehow.

I jump

with a vain grin on my face because I fly for the

moment.

Peppermint Sally

Joseph needed a simple. His entire thirty-six year old life was spiraling all into hell and he was past the point of seeking answers. Joseph Helms needed a simple. A simple problem, for once. A simple solution. A simple something. Everything had always seemed extraordinarily complicated for his weary mind, and things, no matter how wonderfully they had begun, always, inevitably, turned foul.

Recently, his wife of seventeen years, Helen, had fallen ill and was bedridden with intermittent high fevers, smallpox like marks, and general complaints of dizziness and fainting spells. No one knew exactly what

71

she had, but of course, everyone had an opinion. The doctors and specialists had come around for three days, (paid of course by her concerned relatives,) debated amongst each other for another two days, and finally, concluded nothing. The pungent smell of sterilization offended Joe's sensibilities about how a person should live, so when the doctors were around he conveniently left to run errands; straight downstairs to the local whore, Peppermint Sally. Joe had stopped visiting as a paying customer years ago when he got married, and would come down to Sally's just to talk things out. Occasionally, Sally would service Joseph 'on the house', seeing as he was so neighborly. But he always made sure to never ask because he thought it would be immoral for him to ask, since he was married.

Joe knocked on Sally's hardwood door. Her door

felt thicker than all the other doors in the apartment complex.

"Hold on!" Sally's voice screamed.   Listening intently, Joe faintly heard some kind of shuffling. Sally's voice spoke again, this time more quietly.   "You sure that thing's workin'? You better hurry it up."

"Listen," Joe said through the door, "I'll just come back later."

"Oh Joe! Is that you? Come on in."

Joe slowly opened Sally's door, walked through her minuscule hallway, and reached the doorway of her bedroom.   Inside, Sally was just placing a peppermint from the bowl on the small cabinet to the left of her bed, into her mouth. On top of her was William Peters, local Construction Chief Union #693, banging away like a jackhammer.   Having experienced this same situation

73

several times before, none of the parties involved spared the time to even attempt to look embarrassed. Sally sucked at the peppermint and then loudly swallowed her saliva.

"Problems?" she asked. She lay flat on her back, legs high in the air, letting Peter's peter do all the work. A loud crunch was heard as Sally sucked her peppermint again and then bit it in half. Joe caught himself admiring her still fairly shapely body. He had momentarily indulged in a daydream about being lodged between her powerful legs.

Joe righted himself and said, "Yeah, Helen's feelin' real poorly. She's all light in the head, got some kinda spots appearing and disappearing all over her, and's runnin' a fever high into the hundreds." At that, William Peters let out a strained moan. He jammed

Sally one more time, for good measure, and then rolled off with a pleasantly satisfied look on his face. "Wish I felt like that," Joe muttered.

"You can honey," Sally answered, taking Joe by surprise. Right then, he was busily thinking about his life's dire straits and hadn't meant his comment to be heard aloud. Sally got out of bed and went to the bathroom while William Peters slowly put his clothes back on, construction hat last, being extra careful not to zip up his now limp peter in his work pants.

"No, not like that," Joe said. "I mean satisfied."

"I know what you mean, Joe Helms," Sally said.

"Listen Joe," Peters said before he left, "we'll be needin' ten more able-bodied men down at the site come Monday morning. We landed ourselves a contract with the Rockefellers; ya interested?"

"Yes sir!" Joe said to Peters' back as he exited the apartment. He hadn't been able to find decent work since April 15th, 1931, over five months ago. That food line stuff is getting old, Joe would always think to himself as he and his wife would sit down to a meal of cold chicken, peas, creamed corn, and his favorite torture device: Processed Cheese. At least it killed the rats though.

Sally came back out of the bathroom wearing a silky negligee. On, you could see everything she had, and this excited Joe even more than seeing her completely nude. She was the only woman, outside of the new Sears & Roebuck catalogs, that Joe knew who could afford a negligee.

The longer the bathroom door stayed open, the more the bedroom smelled like peppermints, or after-dinner mints. Joe hadn't had an after-dinner mint in a long time, not since he was little and his dad would bring them out after he lit his nightly cigar... He wondered if that was a perfume that Sally wore, or was it a natural occurrence from eating so many mints. He really didn't care; it just reminded him of his past and of an easier life.

"Ya know, that Mr. Peters, he's a real okay sorta guy."

"He is, huh?" said Sally, counting the money that was left for her in the peppermint bowl. It was three dollars short. She uncrossed her legs and lay flat on her bed, after stashing the new money with the rest under the mattress.

"Yeah.   He said I can start on with the construction team Monday morning."

77

"You in the union?" Sally asked.

"No... Crap, your right! I better go do that early tomorrow morning." Joe hadn't thought about that. "I know I got the skills, though. They better let me in."

"They'll let you in," Sally reassured him, "I'm sure of that. Heck, I'll even pay your first dues for ya, with five percent interest, of course."

"You're one hell of a lady, Sally."

"Don't I know it."

Everything seemed to be looking a lot better to Joe after he'd come done to Sally's. "How 'bout something for me?" Sally asked and slowly started removing her negligee. Who was Joe not to oblige such a fine young lady? Life seemed almost easy, less complicated. Simpler. "A freebie," Sally said and reached over for a peppermint as Joe mounted her.

East Coast

Like steam rising from a coffee cup

The oak sprouts leaves early in spring.

First a flourish, to indicate its heat,

And then, only sporadically;

Signifying its willingness to be sipped.

Sweep Up

when I fall

watch out!

the heights I've attained

leave room for quite a bang

when I fall

it's not so bad

when the floor's been swept

the trash has been bagged

the big easy

allows me the freedom

to fall, and fall, and fall

and, somehow, rebound

as I visibly sink

people ask me why I stay

shouldn't I just give it up?

suicide by suggestion

Snakes of Snow

Snakes of snow crisscross the windswept highways of

Upstate New York

They dance beneath the wheels of rental cars and family

vans, alike

Though it's past Winter, far into middle Spring

elsewhere

These icy beasts slither from the thousand islands past

the edge of Lake Ontario

Native to Canada, they seek new territory south

Stealing glances skyward at the migratory birds returning

from their Winter respite

To trace their path back towards the unsuspecting

vacationers

Expecting nothing other than warmth below

escalators

I spied the light of the last

early morning train

reflected off the quiet curve

of the hollow tunnel

and suddenly my mind knew

that it must manufacture

a lost energy, a forgotten spark

to re-animate my limbs

and set them into inevitable motion

like the sleepy

European escalators

that lay dormant

until awoken

by the shuffling,

the staggering,

the prancing,

or the dancing

of many feet,

young or old, this way or that

these new metal stairs

are very charitable, very democratic

they happily accommodate one crowd

by moving up toward the roar of the street

and then pacify the next

by moving down into the chilly depths

alone, they wait patiently

to spirit along the next

great wave,

or even the single commuter

wondering why he never

feels another soul close to his

own.

Mrs. Lybin in the Playroom

Matt's mother did strange things all the time. I noticed this, but when I told Matt he told me that I shouldn't mention it anymore. It was just menopause or something like that. All I remember is that it was some word that I didn't know or care about.

At first, whenever I came over, she would be staring at their large twenty-six inch television. She very rarely looked up and when she did it was only to make a groaning sound in the back of her throat like the gathering of mucus. She never spit though. Matt and his father seemed not to notice, but it always bothered me. I didn't like being around her much when she was like that so Matt and I spent most of the summer in his tiny little yellow playroom at the back of the house.

Matt was the youngest of eight children in the Lybin's family so his parents were pretty old. Well, very old, in comparison to mine. Matt's oldest brother Thomas was thirty-two; three years older than my mother. It always weirded me out to think that Matt's parents, the parents of my nine-year-old friend, were also old enough to be my parents' parents.

One day Matt and I were wrestling in his playroom and practically tearing down what it had taken his dad seven children to finally build right, (his dad liked to brag about his carpentry skills by always bringing up the playroom), when his mother burst in. She had large milky tears in her eyes, as if someone had been squeezing her by the neck, and she was clad in nothing but a bra and support panties. Remarkably, for a woman of her age she had a very handsome figure and her breasts were still large and firm. Her gray hair lay across her face in mats and mingled with her tears.

Matt and I were motionless, gripped in each other's arms and legs like a statue. For a moment I wanted to laugh; but I didn't. I looked into Matt's eyes for guidance but nothing was there. He was terrified. I could feel his fear literally gripping me and pulling my hair out. My small, almost inaudible, "Ouch," let the air out of the balloon. 'You're young; too young to understand! Just wait! Just wait 'til you're old! Old and dysfunctional! Can't function, can't eat, can't sleep, can't do anything..."

She stood in the doorway, bleary eyed and jabbering. Blurting out things we couldn't even hope to understand. I didn't know what to do. I didn't know what to think. My mother had told me once that a woman, during her childbearing years, must shed an egg once every month by bleeding and that's why she used those maxi-pads and dad didn't, so I couldn't fathom why the end of all those bloody months would make anyone hysterical. I'd be happy if I was a woman in that situation. No more need for birth control or those clumsy pads, would be a time for rejoicing. Matthew's mother didn't seem to follow in the celebration.

Five minutes of explosion had passed before Matt gained the courage to scream for his father. Three screams later, his dad arrived with a very worried look on his face. As quickly as he appeared, Matt's mother was quiet. Matt's father never even glanced at us, but instead he just silently and carefully placed his arms around her shoulders and slowly walked Mrs. Lybin back into the main part of the house.

After untangling ourselves, Matt and I sat on opposite sides of the playroom, not speaking. What was there to say? Matt's mom had just entered the room in her underwear, screaming. It was the strangest thing I had ever seen.

"That was the strangest thing I have ever seen," I accidentally whispered aloud.

"Me too," Matt replied. Good, at least he understood where I was coming from. "Wow. I didn't know that my mom had such nice tits." Even after knowing him for three years and knowing all of the perverted things he thought and did, that statement about his own mother's tits surprised me. Matt was a weird kid.

it takes all flavors

now, when the alarm sounds

and the big voice says

take cover, take cover

i.d.f., i.d.f.

shelter in place, shelter in place

don i.b.a., don i.b.a.

I push the smashed peas

to the side of my plate

and concentrate on the round ones,

and the mushrooms.

I make sure all the silvery

skin and scales

are off of the back of my

baked fish before I bite down.

sometimes, I'll even give

the local man scooping ice cream

into our awaiting plastic bowls

a knowing look,

a quiet nod,

acknowledging the attack

from his people outside of our fences

letting him know that I know...

of course it is

It's no indictment of you

You're just different

Different from me, that is

Different from what I'm used to

Different from those I know

Different from those I'd wished to know

Different places you've seen

Different people you've known

Different foods you've eaten

Different lessons you've learned

I've learned not to pass judgment

But that's no indictment of you

THE WORLD

I spit

Like a pit

Viper

Venomous bile

All over

Only to protect myself

From the world

Around me.

As the alpha predator I am constantly

Pursued.

Your Mission

With motherhood as your shield

You descended into the night

By choice,

This was now your life.

Hoping to find

Someone not legally lost

You slice your way

Into areas where you're not wanted.

Runaways are running

From something

But you can't, you won't,

believe it's you.

Mothballs

"Psst, David, are you okay in there?" I heard her ask.

"Yeah. Just a little cramped, that's all," I said.

"Well stop snoring then!" Fergie said. She was whispering but I could tell she was concerned. I was notorious for snoring after a night of serious drinking, and that last night definitely counted as serious. I'm not sure that I ever left the keg's side.

Anyway, afterwards, just like every other weekend night for the last month, I inhabited Fergie's closet. I occupied my space along with seven pairs of dress shoes, two pairs of tennis shoes, three pairs of sandals (two of which I bought her) and the hanging bottoms of countless dresses. Many of the dresses I never saw anywhere else but the closet. The shoes were positioned underneath my folded legs and the dresses hung precariously above my reclining head. One wayward flinch in the night and all of them could come crashing down. Several times each night I was sure that I'd had it; I would drown in dresses. Luckily, or unluckily, that never happened.

As I lay in the closet, only occasionally adjusting myself to avoid cramps and pins-and-needles, I started to think. Why was I in this closet? It was dusty and dark, with only a small glimmer of light able to penetrate from underneath the door. I never accomplished anything with this train of thought though, as I usually went back to my dreams within five minutes. To dream meant not feeling the pain of staying in one constant position.

My dreams always began rather pleasantly - in fact they usually mirrored the beginnings of the night. Fergie and I would arrive at her house at one o'clock a.m. and while she went inside to make sure her parents were asleep and to turn off their alarm clock, I would hide outside behind her family's gray Chevy Suburban and her father's prize possessions - his two fishing boats. I waited there, counting mosquitoes, until I heard the key turning to their side door. When she opened it, I would enter, and this was the usual start of our well choreographed weekend rendezvous.

Then mysteriously, but with utmost regularity in my 'closet' dreams, I would become Fergie. After I removed my long blonde hair from my eyes I would carefully lock the door behind us. "Do you want to brush your teeth?" I would always ask. I could never go to bed with dirty teeth. I would enter the bathroom with David, me, behind me. As I turned to close the bathroom door I noticed that David was already staring at my ass. "Calm down," I'd whisper. I would always brush my teeth, wash my face, and brush my hair first and while David did this I would slowly run my hands up and down his chest, feeling every muscle.

"Do you want to take a shower?" David would ask.

"Yes," I would say. Not 'sure', but 'yes'. I liked being nude next to him and I knew that he knew that I did. While kissing we would slowly undress each other, making sure not to make any noise with falling shoes, belt buckles, or anything. Then we would enter the shower, him first, well me first, so I could play with the minute black hairs which covered his entire backside. They seemed like and undiscovered jungle waiting to be explored. Leave my butt alone he would say with a smile and a laugh, and swat my hand away. I loved that smile.

After the shower we took turns drying each other and we both seemed overly gentle, not wanting to touch certain areas of each other's bodies. We had to pat ourselves down with the towels, supposedly already being dry. Then, just as mysteriously and regularly as before, I would become myself again, in time to make love with Fergie in the only way I knew how - as a man.

But one day something seemed to change within me as I slept in Fergie's closet. I didn't return completely to my own persona in the dream and I made love to myself. It seemed mystical. I awoke with a strange burning sensation in my gut. It was anxiety about the impending conversation which was necessarily going to take place.

"David? I think my parents have left. You can come out now."

I unwound myself and Fergie gave me a hand out of the closet. She returned to her bed and lay there with nothing on except for the lace panties she had gotten as a present from her friend Jennifer.

"Are you going to lie down?" she asked. "You can stretch out now, you know."

I sat down on the edge of her daybed, staring at

the side of her face which wasn't smothered deep in her pillow. "Why do I have the penis?" I asked her.

"All the better to place condoms on," she said in a comical baritone voice.

"No, I'm serious," I said. "I mean, I love you very much, but sometimes I wish you were the man and I was the woman. Don't you want to know what it's like to be on the other side of the fence? I could spend my whole life thinking up different sexual positions and all I would basically be doing is the same thing; well, almost."

She sat up at that and placed her hands on my shoulders as if to feel that I was all there.

"I've been having strange dreams in your closet," I said. "Dreams about making love to myself. Not masturbation, or anal sex, or anything, but full fledged sex with myself, and liking it." I couldn't think of any other way to explain it. She didn't look as stunned as I expected.

"Maybe the mothballs have affected you somehow," she said and started pressing one hand against my forehead.

Mothballs... affected me somehow? She was grasping for straws; or moths maybe. I had never even smelled any mothballs in Fergie's closet. A high enough concentration to affect a person would have an extreme smell, right?

"No, it definitely wasn't the mothballs," I said harshly. Her dam burst very rapidly.

"I don't know what to say," she said. Then she started heaving and wailing uncontrollably. Her breasts felt large and firm against me.

"I love you," I reassured her. "I don't know what I'm even saying. Maybe I've just sat in there too long."

I left her house that morning with a nebulous feeling of disgust and failure because Fergie hadn't understood my troubles and neither had I. Only years later did I figure out that those dreams were my subconscious mind trying to help me understand that I was just like every other high school boy sleeping with his first. It was the sex I wanted, not necessarily her. My feelings for her were deep and true, but I think I already knew that our relationship couldn't last. We had this time to explore and experiment with each other and nothing more. I had overdosed on my desire and imploded our relationship, but my destruction seemed also to involve one blissfully unawares of my dangerous love.

Not Really an Understudy

while I am away

you are me

you are still you

but you also represent me

in all of your actions,

in your day-to-day activities

when I return

I am both proud and slightly embarrassed

that you were a better me

than I ever really was

my death

from my failing eyes

too tired to relay

the correct information

anymore

I follow the movement

of your lips

my mind swirls

as you mouth

what I have always

wished to hear

my ears, so old, too old,

don't dispute

your beautiful, translucent

words

it is only my hands,

my accursed, abused, and arthritic fingers

that deliberately

seek out and touch

your moist mouth

they tell me of your warm, fervent breath

and how it speaks of the ugly

and inevitable truth

STRINGY HAIR, ACNE

She has sacrificed

Herself to write

All other considerations are forgotten

She gingerly rolls on her back

Exposing the soft underbelly

She giggles when

We tickle and scratch

She squeals when

We poke and pierce

Letting her insides, out

We say,

"There, there... you'll

Be okay.

We'll take care of you."

But everyone already

Knows that she's

Destroyed

everything's temporary

I've learned my lesson

as hard as it was

but, at least, it was here

far away from my normal life

here, no one I really care about

will see me fail, see me shamed, see me cry

far away from my everyday

why should I care

if I fall on my face?

the plane ride back home

will give me time to heal

prop me up once again

straight and tall will I exit

my weakness left

thousands of miles away

Incessant Rain

Walter hoped to find meaning hidden somewhere within the night's rain. Here, it was always raining, no matter what the weather. It was a constant steady downpour, interrupted only by strong gusts of wind or short lapses where the water droplets would become as hard as hailstones.

Tonight the rain wasn't so bad. Walter easily dodged the puddles and only occasionally would a rather cold raindrop fall past his damp hair and into his collar. A small brown girl, obviously still early in her school years, dropped her neatly folded paper bag in fright as Walter quickly shivered by. His sudden movement pleased Walter in two ways: it threw off the grip of the cold rain, and it apparently startled the little girl. Walter liked it when he frightened the brown people. It was only fair; they always frightened him. They would gather together on his local street corners, absorbing all the light, bringing eternal night to his once bright neighborhood. He felt like he was walking down the street with his eyes closed. Everyone and everything was dark, and anything could leap out from the darkness and harm you.

Things weren't always so murky for Walter Driggers. He just couldn't seem to remember exactly when they weren't. His memory was the most clouded thing around him. It caused a constant palpable haze, which although it confused Walter, also gave him a lazy feeling of protection. He gathered his old jacket collar closer to his neck, fingered the still tender scar located directly beneath his earlobe, and walked on through the steady rain.

At the next corner Walter stopped. "Goddammit!" he yelled into the dark street in front of him. "Goddammit... I can't hope to get acrossed that." Walter stared helplessly into the water filled street. This new river was blocking Walter's path, with both sides of the torrent barreling towards a large ditch, which appeared to be cut right down the center of the roadway. Walter stood and stared, wiping the moisture away from his forehead and placing some of his stringy brown hair closer to his eyebrows in hopes of further concealing his rapidly receding hairline. The scar on his neck throbbed again causing Walter to flinch and grimace instinctively.

"What's wrong Hurricane Walter?" a child's voice

asked from beneath him. Walter stumbled backward, uncontrollably falling against the wooden corner of an abandoned building. He was stunned only momentarily, but long enough for the rain to subtly harden and pelt his exposed face with piercing hailstones.

The child reached out his hand in service as he moved closer to Walter. "Are you okay?" he asked. The child was another brown person, and by his voice, which was still high pitched but obviously strained for better control, a boy of considerable intelligence.

"Again you've hurt me," Walter mumbled to himself, "This new bump on my head is just one more sign... Stop reaching out to get me..." He grumbled on and on, but the boy kept his arm stretched out towards Walter. Finally, Walter grabbed the boy's hand in disgust and pushed it away from his face. The child stepped back and into the glow of a nearby street lamp. Enshrouded by the glare, his face was nothing more than one big, black, amorphous blob to Walter. It seemed to reach out forever into the night and mingle, ever so slightly (but not so faintly as to escape Walter's attention), with the hailstones. "Stay away!" Walter suddenly blurted out, consumed by mounting terror as his protective haze slowly began to fade. Walter's arms crossed over his face, and his dark eyes retreated inward to the furthest recesses of their sockets.

The child, calm as ever, stepped closer to Walter. Only his eyes and his large, tooth-filled smile were visible on his all too black face. "I know it's raining again, isn't it Walter?" the child said. He looked around to get the attention of the crowd on the corner and motioned with his left hand for someone to come over. No one moved an inch from their everyday posts. He turned back to Walter. "It's raining quite alot right now Walter," he said. Walter thought the brown child sounded vaguely familiar. Not the voice itself, but the words.

He sat upright on the pavement, letting his arms fall away from his head, a combination of courage and bewilderment suddenly giving him the will to move. "No, it's not raining," he said. Then he crossed his arms and shivered.

The boy said, "Oh, this is a hailstorm isn't it?" and also shivered.

"How do you know?" Walter asked.

"You told me yesterday that you thought it would hail today, Walter."

"Did I?"

"Yes, you did. I'm Nathan remember? Nathan Simmons. I live right up the block."

Nathan wasn't by any means a small boy. At five feet six inches, and aged eleven years, he was taller than most of the boys in his neighborhood. His wiry frame was draped by an oversized Polo shirt that looked like a dress to Walter Driggers. He couldn't tell if the boy was wearing shorts or not. Nathan reached his hand back out to Walter who reluctantly accepted. He stood up very slowly and deliberately pulled Nathan's face as close to his as possible without physically coming into contact.

"Do I like you?" Walter asked. His breath tumbled outward like a solid object or thick liquid slowly settles to the bottom of clear water. "Do I like you?" he repeated. Nathan remained quiet, quickly flexing the muscles of his nose in an effort to rid himself of the smell of week old human wastes.

Then Walter did something that surprised even himself. He placed his slightly mustachioed lips directly onto Nathan Simmons' lips, and tried to give him an unwanted openmouthed kiss. Nathan immediately plunged his left knee deep into Walter's groin. While Walter was still curled up on the ground whimpering, Nathan kicked him as hard as he could in the center of his chest. Walter laid on the concrete for several minutes trying to catch his breath before Nathan ran down the block to the permanent group of stationary people.

Hurricane Walter was not a young man. The old bones in his chest felt caved in all the way to his heart. Why wouldn't anyone let an old man try to be nice,

123

sweet, or delicate? All his life he encountered nothing but rejection. Girls, women, boys, men, mother, father... When did it stop? He couldn't distinguish between the physical and mental pains anymore.

He couldn't catch his breath.

Nathan ran back to where Walter was laying on the sidewalk. He brought along a boy from the neighborhood named Darren Stubbs. Darren was the only boy in the area who was Nathan's age, but larger built. He was already beginning to develop early, solid muscles and he had a known mean streak. He could afford to within the scope of his pre-teen reality. No one could convincingly oppose him.

Darren kicked Walter immediately without uttering a word. A tiny 'whoosh' of air escaped Walter's steadily parted lips. "I'm gonna take his wallet since he's already down there," Darren said.

"Hurricane Walter doesn't have any money. If he did he'd just spend it on drugs anyway. You know that."

"Well, I'll take 'em and sell 'em then."

Walter's jacket was rough to the touch, like a weather beaten old carpet. Inside the right side pocket Darren found an already used syringe with the tip of the needle broken off. The bit of needle still there was bloody.

"Gross," Nathan said, "put that back."

"Okay. Okay. Hey, when do you think he'll get up? We kicked him alot and he's on drugs..."

"Probably won't be for a long time, why?"

Darren raised the palm of his hand skyward and slowly looked to the heavens. "Well, I just felt a little

125

drizzle. I'm gonna go home so I don't get wet."

Nathan looked at the sky and took notice of the dark clouds that had formed overhead. Then he looked down at Walter who lay perfectly still on the pavement. He wasn't even gasping for air like he was before. Nathan felt slightly sorry for Walter. Darren was wondering why they were still standing over something that smelled so bad.

"I'm glad Walter likes the rain," Nathan said over his shoulder as he and Darren trotted back down the street. "I hope I never end up like him."

the consequence of flirting

mornings,

while you serve me

meats, eggs, grits

I see you work

sweaty, tired, no make-up

you flirt with me

from behind the grease

and you're sexy.

but tonight,

when I just caught

a glimpse of you

127

with your man,

you were made up,

had on tight jeans,

hips showing,

a tight shirt,

nipples showing,

a pink, bedazzled hat

all could see

what an incredible body

you possess...

but it was not sexy

to watch you slink away

head lowered,

afraid your man

might detect our invisible,

unspoken, bond.

Munich Too

the subway tunnels

beneath the city

are clean and cool.

a light wind always

blows through them.

the schedule and route

information

is always conveniently posted,

and correct.

connecting lines of buses

and streetcars are noted.

right now you can buy a monthly

ticket with which you can ride

anywhere within the city limits

for 59 Deutschemarks --

no one ever checks if you have a ticket.

a five meter by three meter

video monitor plays cartoons and

commercials while you wait for

your train

everyone is extremely interested

in what you have to say if

you're an American.

I'm starting to like this place.

a child's poem

"A blackbird trapped among doves longs for a darker
day."
"A blackbird trapped among doves longs for a darker
day."

To this line I bow my head in utter shame

knowing that a small, innocent child is to blame

for my feeling less of a man than I am

This was the first line of the first poem

that that child had ever written

and it means more to me

132

than the combined weight of thousands of my own words

"A blackbird trapped among doves longs for a darker

day."

My writer's skin is microthin no protection from the

world whatsoever

That child's skin is as thick as alligator hide

from birth he already knows the words.

endangerment and enlightenment

cradled by the thick oak's branches

Susan told me:

"dangling midst the moss

There is

A tiny, bright speck of

infinity."

She prodded me

To reach for it

in her not-so-feminine way

and I tried… retrieving it.

but it was only

ever moss

for me.

Moses and the Rolling Stones: Princes of Mediocrity

Moses supposes his toes are roses,

But Moses supposes erroneously,

For nobodies toes are posies of roses,

As Moses supposes his toes to be.

--   Common Pink Elephant Card in

            Passout® the board game

Moses was back from Miami, Florida for his brother's birthday/Halloween party. He was excited to be back because he wanted to tell all of his friends in New Orleans about his recently formed band and their tremendous, and immediate, luck. Playing well together is one thing, but even Moses had to admit that it was just dumb luck that a record contract landed right in their laps, after forming the band only six months earlier. He still wasn't quite sure how it happened himself. One of the other members worked the whole deal out, and Moses wasn't one to quibble with insignificant details.

"Man, Mtume, is it rockin' in Miami," he said to me.

"Yeah, it must seem pretty dull to be back in N.O. after that. I mean, here it's the same old faces doing pretty much the same old thing," I said and refilled both of our beers at one of the five tapped kegs.

"It's only the same old thing if you haven't been gone for seven months."

"True. I guess I missed the place last year myself," I said.

A soft finger brushed the small hairs across the base of my neck.

"Aren't you Mtume Thompson?" a young girl, about sixteen or seventeen, short brown hair and extremely smooth and tanned skin, asked me. Her navy blue tank top with its large white polka dots didn't reach down to the point where her rich-soil colored, oversized shorts began, leaving her entire midriff exposed. The supple leather of her shoes matched her hair and eyes perfectly. Following her lead, I placed both of my hands on her hips and hoisted her high into the air. Surprisingly there wasn't even the slightest strain on my arms.

My meanest look appeared on my face and I said in a menacing growl, "Yeah, what of it?"

"I'm Gabriella," she said. She looked as calm as

138

ever. "John Tucker introduced us once before at Charity's Bar & Deli." I placed her carefully back onto the floor, making sure to keep one hand on her hip as I bent down to speak.

"Oh, I remember you now," I said feeling rather foolish for not recollecting such a beautiful person. "Weren't you and John going out?"

"Just dating. But that's ancient history. You look different; bigger."

"That's just probably the Army t-shirt. You look really nice, though. I especially like the way your shoes match your hair so nicely."

Gabriella bent downward for a moment, and I felt slightly guilty for enjoying such a cheap thrill, then suddenly she leapt up, screaming, "We're wearing the exact same shoes. Isn't that weird?" I looked down and we did indeed have on the same shoes, exactly, except of course for their sizes. "Let's go sit outside on the porch," she said. I turned around to tell Moses where I was going, but he had already wandered off to tell someone else the good news about his band. Thank you, Moses.

Outside, on the porch in front of the house, we commandeered a private corner away from most of the other party goers, and sat down, her between the house and I. We looked into each others eyes for a moment, and strangely enough, I felt awkward, even though I was four years older than Gabriella and had been in one-to-one situations many, many, times.

Gabriella laughed for no particular reason and then abruptly stopped. "You know," she said, "my English IV teacher talks about you all the time."

"Really?" I asked, genuinely stunned and mildly flattered. She moved closer and placed her head upon my shoulder.

With her eyes closed, and her slow, sensuous breathing mesmerizing me, she said, "Sure. He says, 'Mtume Thompson was one of my best students; a very outspoken young man. He, most likely, could have gone to any college he wanted, and he picked L.S.U., my Alma Mater.' He uses you as his, 'Go to L.S.U. and still be a successful person,' example."

"That's pretty funny," I confided with her, "considering I dropped out of L.S.U. after my freshman year. The classes were just too uninteresting."

"Boring, you mean."

"That too." We both laughed in unison, acknowledging the inanity of our conversation. The fascination I had for her childish brand of charm had me perplexed.

Gabriella lay against my shoulder, silently, for five minutes then opened her eyes, sat up, and gave me a very tantalizing peck of a kiss with her moist lips. "Walk me to the bathroom," she said and grabbed me by the wrist as she stood up. We went into the party, into the long and narrow hall with the hat collection, and saw the twenty person line formed outside of the bathroom. Gabriella placed a Chicago Cubs baseball cap from the hat collection, onto my head. "I'm not waiting in this line," she declared, "come with me out back."

Out of the back screen door, we both stepped, and into the very well lit backyard. Moses' brother had once mentioned to me that his landlady was deathly afraid of burglars and had had automatic lights installed at the back of the house. Gabriella didn't care one bit. She took off her top, her bra, her shorts, and her panties, leaving on only her shoes and socks, and handed them all to me. I didn't move one muscle to stop her; only making sure the kitchen door was closed.

She was gorgeous. Her perfectly tanned body, which I now supposed was her natural skin color, appeared to be untouched by human hands. Not one blemish was anywhere on her well shaped and well endowed, body. No matter what part of a girl's body you liked over another, you weren't disappointed with Gabriella. She walked with nonchalance to the middle of the yard, smiled at me, squatted, and began taking a piss. She smiled and pissed for what seemed an impossibly long time. Finally finished, she came back to me to retrieve her clothing. "Thanks for protecting me," she said. "You're welcome," I replied, "No problem." We kissed a long time then, and I felt a bit strange kissing a girl after she had just used the bathroom outside, but that feeling quickly vanished from my mind as I concentrated on her cool tongue and her warm body.

"Who's that sitting in our spot?" Gabriella asked as we returned to our friendly little corner of the front porch.

"Oh," I said sitting down, "that's just Moses. He's alright. Moses this is Gabriella. Gabriella this is Moses."

"Together, we have three of the most interesting names I've ever heard," said Gabriella.

"Moses is the birthday boy's brother. He lives in Miami now, and he's just started a band."

"We've already signed a recording contract with a major label," Moses added.

"Really?"

"Yeah, we start recording as soon as I get back from here. I'm hangin' around until after the Rolling Stones concert 'cause I've already gotten tickets."

I noticed that I didn't seem to be the center of Gabriella's attention anymore.

"Are you going to go see the Rolling Stones when they're here?" she finally turned to ask me.

"The Rolling Stones," I said, "are the crown princes of mediocrity. I wouldn't pay to see them shrunken in a glass bottle." Moses happened to be in the process of standing up at the time and obviously wasn't listening.

"I'm gonna go get another beer," he said and

walked off. Gabriella jumped up after him.

"Where're you going?" I asked her.

"I want another beer too," she said. "Besides, I want to see if I can get a ticket to see the Stones!" She then pranced off into the party. It actually took me a couple of minutes to realize that she wasn't coming back.

The Fighter

This is the New Orleans I remember

The city chilled by a February thunderstorm

After a taxing and chaotic Mardi Gras

Parents at home tending to their children's,

As well as their own, new found illnesses

Brought about by the intense and intentional decadence

A city bright only around its edges

Its heart a ragged center at best, a liquid filled core,

Locals and aliens alike plumbing its depths

For gaudy, forgettable trinkets

New Orleans, rocked back on its heels

By its own riotous beasts,

Content to rope-a-dope along

Saving its energy for a violent twelfth round

Determined to emerge the winner

to my children

I will loose the best of myself

into the void

in order to protect you

from the night

even if this piece of me

is lost forever

covering, cowering, or fighting

I will pay that price

to keep you forever safe.

caught

I caught her

at a coffee shop

at the edge of the Quarter

A competitor's

Her smile gave her away

it seems she uses it on everyone

not just the faithful

at her place of business

When I told her that I was compelled

to turn her in

she leaned in, close and warm

and said, "I was there earlier; working. The coffee's just

better here."

As she laughed and touched my shoulder

we both knew I would never break our confidence.

as close as your town

in far distant lands

bands of renegades roam

home, we keep the peace

seas, terrible and dark

park our ships at their docks

rocks and corral briefly escape the waves

brave men and women

heaven sent, fighting the sea.

as close as your town

round the backs of abandoned shells

dwell husks of men

152

when they expired is a mystery

history lets them slip by the wayside

hide and seek with humanity

vanity helps us not see

we always let them play their games.

when the rains come

scum and filth washed away

day fades behind cool clouds

loud claps of thunder

under distant bridges echo

let go of your lust for sun

one day you'll pray for rain

pain of heat unbearable

at last when day of judgment comes

fun and laughter far behind

find your way into the light

night lasts infinitely longer

stronger, imprisoning your body and mind

kind only to the wicked

pick it and suffer eternally

externally; separate from all others.

A Loss of Professionalism

Reality was just beginning to sink in with Tom. There apparently, was no hope in saving his relationship with Veronique. She had it in her mind to be aloof, and to go out with just one person wasn't puzzling or mysterious enough for her tastes.

As Tom stood in his doorway with the door ajar slightly, he wondered what his next girl would be like. He hoped that by standing there, nude, with only his penis visible through the crack of the open door, the world would know that he wanted an exciting one, a daring one, one who would wake him up in the morning with a black cup of coffee, place the night's sheets in the washer, and then be ready to quickly burst out of the front door and streak around the outside of the house, twice.

It was close to eight o'clock and his lure wasn't working up to his expectations, so Tom decided that he had better put off girl hunting today and proceed to get ready for work like it was a normal day, and not the day after he had relinquished any and all custody of Veronique.

He put on his large black combat boots first, and laced them up tightly. All that was left was his tan overcoat and his extra dark shades. Without the glasses he thought there was a chance that he might be recognized. Once, an old man had stopped him on the street. Tom searched his memory thoroughly but could not place such a distorted face. The man had a huge mole at the corner of his left eye and bushels of hair growing in every direction from his lump-ridden ears. Tom hated both moles and excessive hair.   Carefully, each night, he would pluck any hairs that dared to grow on his chest and check his bathroom mirror for signs of hair re-growth on his head. If he found any he would immediately employ the shears and cut until he was once again bald. The hairy, mole-laden, old man asked Tom for an autograph.

"You must have me mistaken for someone else," Tom said.

"No, I'm sure you're one of the Coneheads, from Saturday Night Live."

"Go to hell, old shit."

From then on Tom decided that if anyone ever asked again, he would give the autograph and not say anything.

Tom Kingston wasn't anyone famous, except in his own eyes. He considered himself much better, much more chic, than anyone he ever came into contact with. No one on his eight-thirty bus to downtown could fill his shoes. Veronique's wanting to see more than one man only served to bolster his pride. She was obviously trying to cover up her deep feelings of inadequacy with Tom. He vehemently believed this. After all, she could never get him to cry out in ecstasy, "Oh, Veronique," the way he could get her to cry out, "Oh, Tom... Oh, God!" Her name was too damn long; it had too many syllables. She wasn't that good, anyway. But he was.

If he wasn't famous just yet, at least he had an

interesting job. He worked as a male model at the Chicago College of Arts and Sciences, and at the University of Chicago. Tom liked working at the University of Chicago much better because he was further away from the leering students who obviously had no talent, otherwise they wouldn't be in class. Besides, the university realized how hard it was to stay motionless while freezing, so they turned the air-conditioner on low.

Having been a nude model for almost a full year now, Tom prided himself on professionalism, and actually thought he brought a bit of respect and class to his workplace. The few, first day of class snickers, was just the inexperience of young, undisciplined artists rearing its ugly head, and were not directed toward any deficiency in his anatomy. He tried to keep himself in

159

tiptop shape. 'A perfect physique -- from head to toe' was his personal motto.

Today Tom happened to be appearing in the raw at the College of Arts and Sciences. His posing area was much closer to the students and it was very chilly. He would do it though, with the same zeal as a Buddhist priest would burn himself in order to fulfill his dharma; or so he liked to believe.

He arrived early and went straight to the instructor's office to get the lesson plan and find out his two prescribed poses. The lesson plan read:

...variation between light and empty space.

1st pose: Lone man reclining, away from

student body (intense shadow)

2nd pose: Man and woman at odds

(Students choice of positions)...

Tom hadn't ever worked with a partner before but he was sure that, at least he, would still be marvelous and unmoving. Leaving the teacher's office, Tom went directly to the class area, disrobed, and practiced his stillness to the utter point of perfection.

The professor of visual arts arrived and set up the lighting while the students filed in behind him. Tom greeted them each with an unconcerned blank stare. He was a professional. The chill seemed to lift somewhat as more and more students entered. In a way Tom was grateful for their presence, and soon all would know of his perfection.

His first pose was relatively easy, with his back turned he received none of the intense light and only had to look at the empty professor's desk and blank wall, as everyone sat in a semi-circle behind him. Fortunately, Tom was granted a twenty-minute break between poses, because his stomach was growling and he wished to grab a small something to eat.

He got dressed and went to the vending machines, where he promptly ran into - Veronique. "What are you doing here?" he asked. "You're not following me around, are you?" He suddenly regretted ever having told her where he worked.

"I wouldn't follow you to a million dollars, Tom Kingston."

"Then what are you doing here?"

"I'll have you know that you are looking at the newest Chicago College of Arts and Sciences model. In fact, I think I'm teamed up with you today."

Tom felt his heart fall into his guts deepest recesses and he limped back to the classroom irrevocably injured. He didn't know if he could do it. He didn't know if he could pose nude with his former girlfriend, and not touch her.

The class picked a classic position with Veronique lying lengthwise on a table facing them and Tom behind her with one leg bent up and his arm reclining on that leg. Five minutes had passed when Tom noticed a sudden change in their pose. "No," he whispered as Veronique's right hand crept up his leg past his knee.

163

"Why not?" she whispered back. Tom could have stopped Veronique's hand as it found the head of his penis and gently tickled its crown, but he had already resigned himself to the same imperfect state as all of those around him day after day.

Without any more encouragement Tom leapt on top of her, in the middle of class, realizing for the first time in his life that he was not going to be a professional. Was there even such a thing, outside of pornographic magazines and film, as a "professional" nude model? Tom immediately forgot all about the professor and the students. He forgot about the dour mood that he had been in since he awoke that morning, and about the old man who had stopped him in the street that one day, who seemed to be trying to make him feel worse about himself than he usually did. He knew that from this point on he would forever lose that air of perfection, but

for the first time in quite awhile, he felt really good.

This is the Way the World Ends

Deep in the Alaskan Wilderness

A lone hunter-gatherer

Secluded, yet satisfied

Leaves his well-kept cabin

In search of food, firewood,

And other provisions.

His fur parka wrapped

Loosely around his chest

He looks to the nearby mountains

To draw his strength and courage.

His body and mind

Will be like those ancient peaks

He tells himself,

Solid and permanent.

He couldn't hear the cries

Of misery and pain

Or the calls

For instant and final revenge

As he slept

In his cold and pristine paradise

Dreaming of a slow-moving creek

And its quiet silvery denizens.

trapped by choice

I have awoken from sixteen years of slumber

only to find that you can live

without really living,

you can breathe

without ever really stopping to take a breath,

without fresh air,

without sunshine,

but who would want to?

who, but the depressed or the truly downtrodden,

would choose to live that way?

choose to be alive,

but trapped?

to be alone (anna's poem)

surrounded

forever surrounded

those like me are few and far between

we're not better

just different

and that difference makes us suspect

to the others

the others who worship

the idiot,

who cater to the lowest

common denominator

they rally together

"We're proud of our ignorance!"

is their battle cry

"Don't rock our boat.

Be quiet and be popular."

but I can't be quiet

their mere presence irritates me

so I would rather be

alone.

A Ferry Ride

Understanding does not lead to comprehension

I understand that the crew-cut girl on the tiny

ferry has a 'Social Problem', her t-shirt says so, but I

cannot comprehend why.

The freight ship Ayiassos silently slips by with

its waterline completely showing and its raised bulbous

port signifying its lost cargo.

Even empty its still tremendous wake rocks our

little ferry.

Great puffs of black smoke spew from the ferry's

stacks as its engines labor to cruise the less than half of a

mile across the river.

The large ferry heads in the exact opposite

direction, dropping its people at the beginning.

We land with a resonant thud at the end.

Two Penny Circles

Your lover's toes wiggle as he sleeps. They annoy you but they're bearable because you love him. You love Jasper Thurnan. You do. At age twenty-eight you finally realize that true love, for Alison Moore, is large, hairy, has a slight sag in the midsection, and actually enjoys working nine-to-five. And it slumbers not two inches from your naked body, toes jerking as violently as a spasm.

Circles have appeared underneath your lover's eye sockets - small, dark areas which seem to drag his eyes, lids, brow, and forehead downward behind them. As he sleeps you place pennies inside the circles,

174

marveling at their size for such an early age. There the pennies become worn and cracked as if corroded. In the morning all that is left of your two cents are tiny bits of copper dust, which Jasper promptly brushes away with a loud, all-encompassing yawn and a sweep of his still powerful hands. Carefully, he cradles your body against his own. Your back and behind touching his chest and groin respectively, knees up, in a dual fetal position.

The omniscient leading the blind, you think, as Jasper lies quietly. How can someone learn about life from someone who's so totally entrenched in it? So secure that by comparison everyone else appears totally terrified of real life, true existence on this plane, and are merely content to skirt along the edges as powerless phantoms who cannot even withstand a simple exhalation of breath by a real human.

"Sometimes you scare me," you say aloud.

His nose tickles your inner ear as he asks, "What?" A tiny shiver creeps downward through your body; he's trying to make you horny, and it's working. You fight it.

"Sometimes you scare me," you repeat. "You seem to have settled quite nicely into this suburbanite lifestyle."

"Don't be fooled, I'm just as insecure about the future as you are."

"Insecure? Do I appear insecure to you?"

"Apprehensive I meant to say. Shush." He pulls you in closer and patiently rubs your stomach and chest all over. It feels good. His massage relaxes you for the moment and you drift back asleep.

Light. White, blinding light destroys your

pleasant dreams about lazy picnics by a mirrored lake. You know it's morning and the sun should be up but the light invades your small bedroom and attacks your face directly. Blinded, you slowly remove the covers from your body and stumble out of bed towards the window. You had planned on closing the curtains but something huge bars your way as the light shines down with even more intensity. You shade your eyes and repeatedly blink until the light merely fills the room instead of obliterating it. Your eyes adjust, eventually, upon Jasper, naked and peering out of the flung open bedroom window, arms spread outward like a vulture about to perch upon a rotting carcass.

"I've decided to quit my job at Avondale and go back to school, Alison," he says turned toward the window; voice as steady as ever. "It just doesn't feel

177

right at the shipyard. It's like I can't relate to anyone around me because I honestly think they're stupid. And I think the feelings pretty much mutual. I'm not at all interested in ship welding so it's hard to pay attention to what I'm doing." Again it's silent in your bedroom. Out of it all, the word 'stupid' lingers in the air, hard as granite, crushing your last little bit of confidence completely out of your semiconscious body. "Well, I just think I could be doing more with my life. I've thought about what you said this morning, and you're right. I'm not a suburbanite; it doesn't satisfy me." Quickly, Jasper turns toward you, his stolid expression portraying the personal depth of his rhetoric. He doesn't want an answer from you, or an opinion -- He's decided already. You just follow.

"On March 29th, 1990, Jasper Thurnan, my lover, quit his five year job at Avondale Shipyards to go back to school," you write in your diary. "This is a decision which is either his first step toward something great, or his first major mistake." At that you close and lock your diary fully intending to get up and start working immediately on getting that shipment of plastic Fantastic Earrings from France delivered on time to your Canadian distributor in Montreal. But something unseen cements you in place. For hours you sit, not really thinking about anything, not really knowing what to even start thinking about. You cry, too. Off and on -- Just out of frustration. You love Jasper, but you hate yourself for it.

At three o'clock the phone rings, waking you up

from hunched over your desk. Inventory sheets fly everywhere when the first ring startles you, but by the fourth you have them all back in order. After ringing for the sixth time you pick up the telephone's receiver, move the hair from in front of your face, and ask the usual question, "Hello?" You notice how your voice flutters when you speak so you swallow several times in order to sound steady.

"Alison," the voice says, "I'm still over at Avondale. I stayed at work all day to make sure I wanted to quit. It's a hard decision, just quitting something you've done for years, but now I'm positive. I'll be back at the apartment by six. Bye." The voice doesn't just fade away in anticipation of a possible reply; it cuts off all future retorts. Why, you wonder. Why so abrupt?

Trying to forget the majority of your troubles you

dive into your work. The clock to the right of you ticks wildly out of control. Every click of its gears flails you deep within the depths of your ears, each eardrum keeping tempo with both the second hand and your heartbeat. Something is wrong, you can feel it. Something about this whole situation is absolutely rotten. Maybe it's the relationship all together. These last few days have really bothered you.

Tuesday the meeting with your newest client went off without a hitch. They accepted every deal that you laid on the table. They even ordered fifty of the 'Purple Ray-Gun Warrior', an earring set that you had been trying to pawn off on someone for the last year straight. They bought eagerly; a little over eagerly maybe. Barbra Hurd, the buyer and owner, of Doctor's Orders, appeared totally preoccupied with something as she made purchases for the trendiest boutique in the Metro Area. She had never been one to buy off-hand, but made selective decisions based on what you figured were months and months of research. But although smiling quite a bit, Barbra was known for this trait after all, she sniffled continually throughout the meeting and rejected any of your inquiries and only mumbled after any of your many conversation starters. She readily accepted any and all orders though. Usually this would have had you ecstatic, a buying spree would have ensued, and Jasper would end up having possibly five new pair of antique wing-tipped, two-toned shoes, complete with moldy smell, which of course you would end up wearing. But not this time. Of any of the purchasers in your circuit of boutiques and curio shops in New Orleans, Barbra, while all business-like, was perhaps your only true friend, your only fellow sympathizer. You had met her previously at a social gathering and you were positive that you two had hit it off perfectly. In fact you immediately felt a twinge of love for this perfect stranger of a woman when you were introduced by a mutual friend. She was everything that you had always wanted to be: beautiful beyond belief, ultra-intelligent, successful, and totally self-made. If she were a man you probably would have forgotten all about Jasper and offered to go to bed with her. Hell, you were still thinking about it.

That mutual friend, Edgar, that you have known since elementary school, had mentioned to Barbra that you were in the import business and she had expressed a desire to meet you, noting that she had started out as an independent importer five years ago shipping extravagant costume jewelry from Guatemala to local Mardi Gras costume outlets. As she told you all about her previous successes, you could tell she didn't want to appear arrogant, and she stopped repeatedly to try and give you advice for climbing up the ladder. "Alison," she said, "you've got to feel free in order to achieve anything. You've got to create the leeway to let your imagination seep into your everyday life. Then opportunities will literally bury you. Life is cyclic you know. One big, mind-boggling circle. What you put out is exactly what you get back. Make an effort; you never know what could happen." It sounds to you like she's trying to urge you to do something.

After thanking her for the free seminar you excuse yourself to go mingle through the other members of the party. As you talk to general acquaintances, and some actual friends, you can feel tightness between your neck and shoulders. It almost feels like someone is watching you, making sure this misfit bull that you feel you are doesn't wreck any of the china.

"Surely you should be paid for the advice you so frequently give to the less fortunate, Barbra," says Edgar obviously trying to be cute and get on Barbra's good side. You can read his lips from across the room as you silently search for the bathroom. It's obviously just small talk, but it hurts to realize that an old school chum now feels that you're not truly on his level anymore. Barbra seems completely disinterested in whatever Edgar has to say and this immensely satisfies you.

Wednesday morning, after a spectacular night of totally lustful sex with Jasper, (he's best on Tuesday nights,) he wakes you up at six a.m. with telephone in hand. It's your mother, worried that her only daughter hasn't called once in the last month. You can't remember very clearly but perhaps you really did tell her that talking to her at six in the morning is just like shaving your pubic hairs for a bathing suit you only plan on wearing for one day. It causes nothing but unwanted irritation.

The rest of the day doesn't go much better. One of your clients calls to tell you that they'll no longer be requiring your services. Economic reasons they say: It's just too hard for them to keep afloat in New Orleans with its ravaged economy. You tell them that you understand completely, thank them for their previous business dealings, wish them luck in all future endeavors, and slowly postpone hanging up the receiver until you're positive that the conversation has just taken place.

"Don't worry about a thing," you say out loud to yourself for reassurance. You'll get through this the same way that you've gotten through everything else, by the hair on your ass.

That night Jasper isn't all too understanding of any of your problems. Of course his problems are all more important than yours. You can stay up all night and comfort him and appear to understand every nuance of anything he says. But it seems to be okay if he falls asleep at the slightest mention of your daily aggravations.

You say to him while he's sleeping, "You know I don't believe any of this better than thou act you play. I know you have the same loves and fears as almost everyone else. I know you worry about our relationship.

187

I know you look at other women and wonder what it would be like to be with them. I know you sometimes wonder about the basis for your sexuality. I know more about you then I let on, and more than you think."

"And maybe less than you think you know," Jasper says and rolls over with a shit-eating grin on his face. He starts tickling you as soon as the vexation appears and reddens your face. Both of you tumble around in bed tickling each other into hysteria for about an hour. Eventually you fall asleep not really satisfied.

Wiggling toes wake you on Thursday morning, and the first thing you are aware of are Jasper's huge, sealed eyes, totally anti-climatic on a face dominated by the black holes which weigh his features down. Inside these you place two pennies from the small table next to the bed.

After that thought you remember to finally get back to financial matters. Balancing the now downtrodden books is all that you can allow on your mind now. After getting out all the appropriate bills you go to the refrigerator, get a beer, and return to your desk. You start writing the required checks: the gas bill, the electric bill, the Visa Charge Card, the AT&T Calling Card... You stop at the rent statement for the apartment horrified and bewildered. On the statement is a small note:

> The rent for this month and the next
>
> is already paid for. I couldn't leave
>
> without doing at least that for you.
>
> Thanks for the extra two good luck
>
> pennies. I hope I don't need them.

I will always love you. Jasper.

more or less

here is more

and more is sometimes better,

sometimes not.

when you're out

in the dark of night

alone

more is a character

you leave at the club's portal,

loud and vulgar

while you strike out

toward your resting

place, and a safe

tomorrow. at the heart

of a new, vibrant city

more acquaints

you with the important

sights, leaving the more

touristy things

to those with less.

more may not be

in sheer numbers

of people

but with volume

more, more than

makes up for it.

An Attack on My Kingdom!

A small note was passed under my door today,

It said that, "It should be noted that several pieces of

post,

Addressed to you, have been recovered from the home of

_____,

A FORMER postal worker..."

It might as well have said that a tunnel had been

discovered under the moat

That rings my castle,

That infiltrators had been apprehended there,

And their diabolical plans revealed!

It was an attack upon my Kingdom!

My realm, my respite, my solitude, had been defiled,

Not by a direct frontal assault,

But by the rather insidious means of rifling through my

mail.

What coward intercepted what was intended for me,

Is not a matter of my concern.

What I have to concentrate on,

Is how I will prevent such breaches in the future,

How I'll keep the enemy from penetrating my gates,

While still maintaining the tranquility of my Kingdom.

Why I Stopped the Dream

We were together for three years

The dream began as a conversation between us,

A planning of our mutual future

When I left physically

She left emotionally,

And then physically,

And then physically, again

As we split

I released the dream to her

Not knowing

That she too had released

The dream as a part of me

Allowing it to fade from her life

Luckily, like an attention starved puppy,

It followed me for decades

Only I was too self-absorbed

To turn, and take notice,

And care

When I finally learned to observe,

To appreciate everything around me,

The dream was there,

My steadfast companion

Weathered, tattered, flea-bitten

Immediately, I determined

To care for and nurture it

To bring it back to full health

No matter that it reminded me of her constantly

It was the good; the beautiful

Part of her that it evoked

The part I had seen return

As a tear in the corner of her eye

When we spoke

One emotionally filled night

At our school's reunion

Before her husband

Wisely interrupted

humans live in cement

maybe at dusk

heaven pouring itself

along the pavement

vegetation may appear

stronger than man's porous casing

shattering its facade of surface tension

maybe, with the sun in concert

the desert will slightly swell

slowly enveloping the man-made oasis.

maybe by the position of the moon

upon the earth's surface

the waters will wash away the waste

whatever happens, be prepared

because things will change.

maybe at dawn

a chorus of bells

waking up the zombies

caffeine to spirit them away

in their rolling metallic boxes

hands gripped tight on the wheels

perhaps with urging from their co-workers

they'll finally walk away

resolve to follow their dreams.

at night, sleeping, they are happy

their dreams tell them that things will change.

THEY WERE HAPPY ONCE

Once, they were happy. They did things together which made each other happy. Everyone that they knew who saw them hand-in-hand, walking down the city streets doing nothing so much as window shopping, commented on their glowing demeanor, and the unusual length of their simultaneous strides.

One sunny day, this day as happy as all others (for almost all of their days were pure joy), as they picnicked under the grandest shade tree in their favorite park, he decided that it was now an okay opportunity to ask his lover about the time before. The time before the happiness. The time they never spoke about.

"We never talk about that time," his lover commented, and noticeably returned to his previous picnic routine.

"I know," he said. How could he bring it up in a non-intrusive way? "That's the problem. I haven't yet put it behind me. It gnaws at my psyche' because we didn't talk through it."

"I don't want to talk through it," insisted his lover. "I don't wish to speak about it at all."

Their joyous picnic day soured, they quickly and quietly packed the food and the blanket into the basket, being careful not to get too close and have the other feel the physical heat of the situation. In the car they each leaned against their respective doors in order to maintain an artificial distance. Better to fall from the moving auto in a freak accident than to concede to rationality.

"We were happy once," he said, offhandedly. His lover drove on, silent and still. "Like the pendulum swings and the seasons change, we will be happy again."

"Do you know why?" he asked.

"Why?"

"Because," he concluded, "despite that time in the past, we have achieved what every couple searches for - the mutual want of permanence."

They drove on in silence. He was satisfied that they had finally talked through that time. His lover was grateful that they had not.

genetic

one of my children hates the dentist,

hating the dentist is genetic, instinctual

don't let anybody tell you differently

Before the Disintegration

In a quieter time

When little girls

Skipped Double-Dutch

On clean, hot, sidewalks

Men without jobs

Probably weren't out looking.

They sat on stone steps

and sweated with pride.

Their polyester hairdos

Were glistening globes of distinction

Which they tended

206

With great care.

They knew it was better

To be slick and beautiful

Than average and square.

game day

to be in Phoenix

late fall

inadvertently receiving a tan

realizing

as if reality

had just arrived

for the first time

in my life

that greatness,

true, lasting greatness,

is but one

fatal, unforgiving step

next to tragedy

next to oblivion

next to despair

next to desperation.

many a vagrant here

bear an unsettling

resemblance

to your favorite

stars

Yesterday in Class

In class I lost myself.

Seated, I escaped upward

through my mind,

hovered,

then plunged under the crack

of the door.

Darris © 1988 by F. Alison Wells

Darris is an Active Duty service member of the United States Armed Forces. He has lived and traveled extensively throughout the United States, Europe, and Asia, for both business and pleasure. Writing has helped him to maintain his sanity while enduring multiple deployments to Iraq and Afghanistan. This is his first collection of stories and poems.